I SEE
SAFARI ANIMALS
A NEWBORN BLACK & WHITE BABY BOOK

BY Victoria Hazlehurst
& Lauren Dick

ENGAGE BOOKS
VANCOUVER

ENGAGE BOOKS

Mailing address
PO BOX 4608
Main Station Terminal
349 West Georgia Street
Vancouver, BC
Canada, V6B 4A1

www.engagebooks.com

I See Safari Animals
I See
Hazlehurst, Victoria 1945 –
Dick, Lauren 1997 –
Edited by: A.R. Roumanis
Designed by: Lauren Dick

FIRST EDITION / FIRST PRINTING

LIBRARY AND ARCHIVES CANADA CATALOGUING IN PUBLICATION

Title: I See Safari Animals: A Newborn Black & White Baby Book /
by Victoria Hazlehurst & Lauren Dick.
Names: Hazlehurst, Victoria, author. | Dick, Lauren, 1997- author.
Description: I See Newborn Black & White Baby Book series.

Identifiers: Canadiana 20210170816
ISBN 978-1-77476-299-8 (hardcover). –
ISBN 978-1-77476-298-1 (softcover). –

Subjects:
LCSH: Animals—Africa—Juvenile literature.

Classification: LCC QL336 .H39 2021 | DDC j591.96—dc23

3 Giraffe

5 Elephant

7 Hippo

9 Cheetah

11 Crocodile

13 Lemur

15 Tiger

17 Lion

19 Flamingo

21 Turtle

23 Monkey

25 Rhino

27 Ostrich

29 Parrot

31 Anteater

33 Hyena

35 Toucan

37 Zebra

39 Meerkat

41 Gorrilla

What do **YOU** see

1

on the safari?

2

I see a giraffe's tall

NECK.

I see an elephant's long

TRUNK.

I see a hippo's strong

JAW.

I see a cheetah's spotty

PRINT.

I see a crocodile's thick

SCALES.

I see a lemur's ringed

TAIL.

I see a tiger's many

STRIPES.

I see a lion's proud

MANE.

I see a flamingo's soft

FEATHERS.

20

I see a turtle's hard

SHELL.

22

I see a monkey's friendly

FACE.

24

I see a rhino's sharp

HORN.

I see an ostrich's powerful

LEGS.

28

I see a parrot's pretty **WINGS.**

30

I see an anteater's hungry

TONGUE.

I see a hyena's tiny

SPOTS.

I see a toucan's large

BEAK.

36

I see a zebra's four

HOOVES.

38

I see a meerkat's small

SIZE.

I see a gorilla's dark

HAIR.

I'll see you **NEXT TIME!**

43

Explore other books at www.engagebooks.com

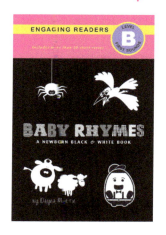

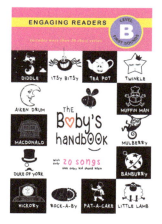

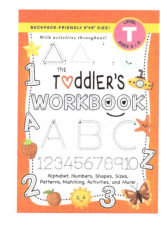

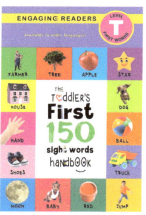

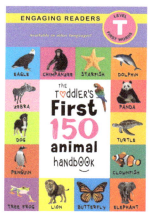

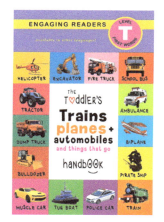

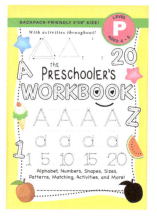

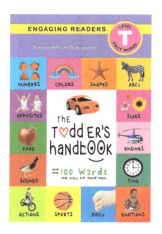

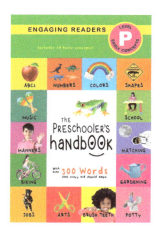